HEINEMANN ELT GUIDED READERS

ELEMENTARY LEVEL

ELIZABETH LAIRD

Eddy and the Movie Star

ELEMENTARY LEVEL

Series Editor: John Milne

The Heinemann ELT Guided Readers provide a choice of enjoyable reading material for learners of English. The series is published at five levels – Starter, Beginner, Elementary, Intermediate and Upper. At **Elementary Level**, the control of content and language has the following main features:

Information Control

Stories have straightforward plots and a restricted number of main characters. Information which is vital to the understanding of the story is clearly presented and repeated when necessary. Difficult allusion and metaphor are avoided and cultural backgrounds are made explicit.

Structure Control

Students will meet those grammatical features which they have already been taught in their elementary course of studies. Other grammatical features occasionally occur with which the students may not be so familiar, but their use is made clear through context and reinforcement. This ensures that the reading as well as being enjoyable provides a continual learning situation for the students. Sentences are kept short – a maximum of two clauses in nearly all cases – and within sentences there is a balanced use of simple adverbial and adjectival phrases. Great care is taken with pronoun reference.

Vocabulary Control

At **Elementary Level** there is a limited use of a carefully controlled vocabulary of approximately 1,100 basic words. At the same time, students are given some opportunity to meet new or unfamiliar words in contexts where their meaning is obvious. The meaning of words introduced in this way is reinforced by repetition. Help is also given to the students in the form of vivid illustrations which are closely related to the text.

Contents

The People and Places in This Story

Eddy Nakamura

Mr Lee

Rosita Marcos

Cathy Chen

Paul Kwok

Su Lin

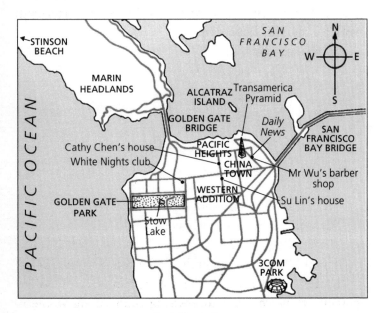

San Francisco

1

A Special Story for Eddy

The office of the *Daily News* was busy. Reporters sat in front of their computer screens. They were writing articles for the newspaper. The door to the chief editor's office was closed. Mr Lee, the chief editor, was having a meeting with all the senior reporters.

Eddy Nakamura sat at his desk. He was not doing anything. He was looking out of the window and he was dreaming of success. He did not notice the busy streets of San Francisco's Chinatown below.

'One day,' he said to himself, 'I'll be the editor of a great national newspaper. And only the best reporters will work for me.'

'Eddy!' someone said.

Eddy looked round. Mr Lee's secretary, Rosita Marcos, was smiling at him.

'Why are you looking out of the window?' Rosita asked. 'Are you writing an article about the sky, or the birds? No? I know what you're doing! You're dreaming about your girlfriend!'

Eddy's face went red. He looked at the floor.

'I don't have a girlfriend,' he said.

'Ah well,' said Rosita. 'If you want a girlfriend, how about me, Eddy.'

'Thanks, but no,' said Eddy. 'I like you, Rosita. But —'

'I know,' said Rosita. 'I'm older than you. But older women are *much* more interesting than young women.' She laughed. 'Don't worry, Eddy. I was joking! You must start your work before Mr Lee sees you.'

Eddy looked at his computer screen and sighed.

'Oh dear,' he said. 'Mr Lee wants me to write about horse-racing. I *hate* horses. Why can't I write about something interesting?'

Rosita smiled at him.

'Mr Lee likes your work, Eddy,' she said. 'He'll give you an interesting assignment soon.'

Eddy tried to write his article about horse-racing. It was very difficult.

An hour later, the door of Mr Lee's office opened. The senior reporters came out of their meeting. Mr Lee looked at Eddy and smiled.

'Come into my office, young man,' he said.

'Yes, sir!' said Eddy nervously.

'He wants to give me a serious assignment,' Eddy thought. 'Perhaps he will give me an important story. '

Eddy sat down opposite Mr Lee. Mr Lee gave Eddy a photograph. The photograph was of a young woman with long black hair and beautiful brown eyes.

'Do you know who this is?' Mr Lee asked.

Eddy looked at the photograph.

'Yes. It's Cathy Chen,' he said. 'She's a movie star.'

'Yes,' said Mr Lee. 'Look at her. She's beautiful, famous and rich. Cathy Chen was born here in Chinatown, Eddy. Did you know that? People here are very interested in Cathy Chen. They want to know about her. They want to know about the clothes she wears, about her cars and about the house where she lives. They want to know about her interests. And they want to know about her private life. All these things. But she doesn't like newspaper

'Do you know who this is?'

reporters and she doesn't give interviews.'

He put the photograph on his desk and looked at Eddy.

'Cathy Chen has a fiancé,' Mr Lee went on. 'His name is Paul Kwok. He was a great tennis player once. He was the number two player in the US. He's much older than Cathy Chen. Why is she going to marry an older man? Perhaps you can find out, Eddy. I want an interesting story about Cathy Chen.'

Eddy nodded. 'OK. I'll try, Mr Lee,' he said.

Mr Lee took some more photographs of Cathy Chen out of the drawer of his desk. He showed them to Eddy.

'Look at these,' he said. 'These are great new photos of Cathy Chen. They are going to be in our new Saturday magazine. All the other papers are going to have colour magazines soon. But we'll be the first, and the best. Eddy, you must write a great story for the new magazine!'

Eddy walked out of Mr Lee's office.

'What did Mr Lee say, Eddy?' Rosita asked. 'Are you going to write a big magazine story? Are you happy?'

'Happy?' said Eddy. 'Of course not. Mr Lee has told me to write about Cathy Chen. I want to write about important things. I want to write *serious* news! I don't want to write silly stories about a movie star.'

'But Eddy,' Rosita said. 'This is your big chance. You must do this story well! Do you understand?'

Eddy sat down at his desk again. He tried to think about Cathy Chen. He did not know anything about her.

Rosita shook her head.

'Here,' she said. She gave Eddy a magazine. 'Look at this. There's a story about Cathy Chen here. The story doesn't tell you much about her, but there's a picture of her new house in San Francisco. Cathy lives there with her aunt. Paul Kwok, Cathy's fiancé, visits her there every day. Why don't you go and look at the house? Perhaps you'll find out something there.'

'Thanks, Rosita,' said Eddy. He kissed her cheek.

'Oo,' said Rosita. 'Is this the beginning of our big romance?'

'No, I'm sorry, Rosita,' Eddy laughed. 'We're just good friends. But thanks for your help.'

He picked up his jacket and went out of the office.

2

In Cathy Chen's Garden

Cathy Chen's house was big. It was at the top of a hill in Pacific Heights. From outside the house, Eddy could see a wonderful view of the Bay below. But he couldn't see the house very clearly. There was a high wall all around the garden and the gates across the driveway were closed.

Eddy stood outside the gates and wiped his face with his handkerchief. It was a hot day.

'I wish that I had a car,' he said to himself. 'If I write a good story about Cathy Chen, perhaps Mr Lee will give me a more interesting assignment. Perhaps he will give me a better job and a car too. Then I'll be able to drive around town. I'll be able to get to important news stories quickly!'

Eddy looked at the front of the house. All the window shutters were closed.

'Perhaps Cathy Chen is away,' thought Eddy. 'Perhaps

she's making a new movie.'

There was a bell and an intercom next to the gates. He decided to ring the bell.

He heard a voice coming from the intercom.

'Who is it?' the voice asked.

'This is Eddy Nakamura from the *Daily News*,' Eddy said. 'Is Miss Cathy Chen —'

There was a click from the intercom. Then there was silence.

'Oh well,' thought Eddy. 'I did try to speak to Cathy Chen.'

He wanted to walk back down the hill. He wanted to have a long cold drink.

'I won't go back to the office yet,' he told himself. 'I must look at her house again.'

There was a small alley between Cathy Chen's house and the next house. Eddy went along it quietly. Soon he was looking at the back of Cathy Chen's house.

Then he saw that a small part of Cathy Chen's wall was broken. Eddy climbed over the broken part of the wall – and suddenly he was inside Cathy's garden!

He looked up at Cathy's house. A window was open. He heard voices. People were talking inside the room.

'This is bad,' Eddy thought. 'I'm spying. This is Cathy Chen's private house.'

He turned to go back to the street. But then he heard a young woman's voice.

'No, Paul! No!' she was crying. 'You never let me do what I want!'

Eddy heard a man's voice. The man's voice was angry.

'Stop, Cathy,' he was saying. 'Stop it at once, or I'll —'

'I'm spying. This is Cathy Chen's private house.'

Eddy heard a crashing noise. Then the woman screamed.

'He's hitting her!' thought Eddy. 'This is terrible!'

Cathy Chen shouted again. Eddy was angry now.

'Poor Cathy!' he thought.

A door banged shut inside the house. Then, for a moment, Eddy saw Cathy Chen at the window.

Suddenly, Eddy heard a noise at the front of the house. A car engine started. He ran back along the alley to the street. Then the gates across the driveway opened and a big black car came out. There were two men in the car – a driver and a passenger.

The passenger was Paul Kwok. He was sitting in the back of the car. His face was angry.

The car turned into the road and drove away quickly.

Eddy walked slowly down the hill. He wanted to write about Cathy Chen now. He wanted to help her.

3

Lucky Eddy!

Eddy went back to the offices of the *Daily News*. In the basement there was a library. The library had a copy of each of the old editions of the newspaper on computer. Eddy sat down at the computer. He started to read the old editions of the newspaper on the screen. He was looking for news about Cathy Chen and Paul Kwok.

The hours passed. Eddy looked at his watch. He was tired, but he was pleased too.

'I understand now,' he thought. 'Cathy Chen met Paul Kwok when she was very young. She was not a famous star then. But Paul Kwok was a famous tennis player. She loved him and she wanted to marry him. But now Cathy Chen is famous too and she's older. She knows more about the world. She doesn't love Paul Kwok now. But Paul Kwok is a proud, cruel man and he wants her. She's afraid of him, and that is why she's going to marry him.'

Eddy stood up.

'Now I have some information about Cathy Chen!' Eddy said to himself. 'I can write a good story.'

He went upstairs. The offices were empty. Everyone had gone home. Eddy sat down at his computer and began to work. At last, his story was finished. Eddy printed a copy of his story. He put the papers on Mr Lee's desk and he went home.

———

The next morning, Eddy came to the *Daily News* offices at seven o'clock. Mr Lee arrived ten minutes later. Eddy watched the chief editor go into his office and he smiled.

'Mr Lee will like my story,' Eddy thought. 'It's good. I know that it is.'

Five minutes later, Mr Lee came to the door of his office.

'Eddy!' he called.

Eddy got up from his chair and went to Mr Lee's office. He was smiling. But Mr Lee was not smiling. He gave Eddy's story back to him.

'You'll have to write a better story than this!' he said. 'We can't use your story! There will be trouble if we put this story in the *Daily News*!'

Mr Lee shook his head. He was angry.

'Anyway,' he went on, 'nobody will believe this story. Remember, Paul Kwok was a big hero – an international tennis star! Why don't you write something about Cathy Chen herself? Write something different. Now go away and start writing. I want a different story on my desk by tomorrow!'

Eddy returned to his desk. He put Cathy's photograph on the wall above his desk. One of the reporters saw it.

'Who's your girlfriend, Eddy?' he said. He looked at the photograph more closely. 'Hey! It's Cathy Chen! Do you like her movies?'

'No, I don't,' said Eddy. 'I have to write a story about her.'

'You're lucky,' the other reporter said. 'I never get nice assignments like that. I have to write about the American Clean Air and Water Convention!'

Eddy laughed.

'I'm not lucky,' he said. 'You are. That's *serious* news.'

The other reporter looked at the photograph again.

'I saw Cathy Chen recently in Sutter Street,' he said. 'She goes to the White Nights Club. Lots of famous people go there. I've seen Cathy Chen go in there several times.'

Eddy smiled.

'Thanks,' he said. 'That's really useful. I'll go to the club tonight. Somebody there will talk to me about her!'

_____

That evening, Eddy went to the White Nights Club. Two large doormen were standing outside the entrance. Eddy waited outside. Some photographers were also waiting. They wanted to take photographs of famous people.

About an hour later, a white limousine stopped outside the club. A woman got out of the car. The photographers ran forward to take photos.

'It's her!' they shouted. 'It's Cathy Chen!'

Cathy went into the club. Eddy tried to follow her but one of the doormen stopped him.

'Members only, sir,' the doorman said.

Eddy turned away. Then he saw the driver of Cathy's limousine. He was standing beside the limousine and reading a magazine. Eddy walked up to him.

'Hi,' he said. 'You're Cathy Chen's driver, aren't you?'

The man looked at him silently.

'Do you go everywhere with her?' Eddy asked. 'Do you go to the film studios, restaurants, parties?'

The man said nothing.

'Is Cathy Chen nice?' Eddy said at last. 'Is she a good employer? Who are her friends?'

The man started reading his magazine again.

'You're a newspaper reporter, aren't you?' he said. 'Only reporters ask silly questions. Well, this isn't your lucky day. You can't interview me. I don't talk to reporters.'

'That's OK,' said Eddy. 'I don't want to interview you. I want to talk to Cathy Chen. I went to her home yesterday. But I couldn't speak to her.'

The driver smiled.

'No, I guess not,' he said. 'Miss Chen doesn't like reporters. And Mr Kwok doesn't like reporters. Miss Chen never gives interviews.'

'What can I do?' said Eddy. 'I have to write an article about Cathy Chen for the *Daily News*. I have to talk to her!'

'You're Cathy Chen's driver, aren't you?'

Suddenly, Eddy had an idea. He took some money out of his pocket. Eddy held the money out to the driver.

The driver took the money and turned to get into the limousine.

'OK, listen,' said the driver. 'Miss Chen likes to walk by the ocean in the evening after coming to this club. She wants me to drive her to Stinson Beach this evening. It's quiet then. Most people have gone home. I'll park the car near the old boat house. You can try to talk to her then. Now go away. Those photographers are watching us.'

Eddy walked away quickly.

'This is my big chance,' he thought. 'I'll go to the beach and I'll try to talk to Cathy. Perhaps she will give me an interview.'

4

At Stinson Beach

Eddy went to the old boat house on Stinson Beach. He waited. The ocean was beautiful in the moonlight. Sea-birds were flying low and their wings were touching the water. The moon made a silver path across the sea. He heard the cries of the sea-birds.

Then Cathy Chen's limousine arrived. She got out of it.

'Stay here,' she said to the driver. Then she took off her shoes.

Cathy Chen began to run. She ran towards some big rocks at the edge of the water. She started to climb the rocks.

'She's going too fast!' Eddy thought. 'She'll fall!'

He ran after her. She was climbing higher and higher. Eddy reached the rocks and he began to climb too.

Eddy was frightened. His heart was beating fast and his legs were shaking. The rocks were wet. Once his foot slipped, and he nearly fell.

Cathy was on a high rock now. She was looking at the ocean.

Suddenly she moved closer to the edge of the rock.

'She's going to jump!' Eddy thought.

'Miss Chen!' he shouted. 'Don't jump! Wait! Let me talk to you!'

Cathy Chen was surprised. She looked down. 'Who's that?' she said.

At last Eddie reached her.

'Please,' he said. 'Please don't jump! Don't kill yourself! You're unhappy now, but things will get better.'

'Who are you?' said Cathy.

'I'm Eddy Nakamura,' Eddy said. 'I'm a reporter. I work on the *Daily News*.'

'You're a reporter!' Cathy said. 'Do you know what I call reporters? Rats. Go away, rat.'

'She's angry,' Eddy said to himself. 'It's good if she's angry. Anger is better than unhappiness. Angry people don't kill themselves.'

'Miss Chen, please,' Eddy said. 'You don't understand. I climbed up those rocks because I want to help you. You're unhappy. I know your fiancé —'

'What do you know about me and my fiancé?' Cathy said quickly.

'You're unhappy,' Eddy went on. 'You argue with him.

18

Cathy was on a high rock now. She was
looking at the ocean.

You and Mr Kwok fight a lot. I want to help you. You must believe me.'

Cathy laughed.

'Do you think that I fight with Paul?' she said. 'If this is true, why haven't you written about our fights in your newspaper? You're a very strange rat!'

Cathy Chen looked away from Eddy. He waited.

'Why are you still here?' she said at last. 'What are you waiting for? Go away, rat.'

'No,' said Eddy. 'I can't leave you here. You're unhappy. You're worried about something.'

Cathy turned to look at him again.

'Worried?' Cathy said. 'Oh, yes, I'm worried.'

She stopped.

'Does Mr Kwok know this?' Eddy asked. 'Can't he help you?'

Cathy shook her head.

'No, I will not tell Paul,' she said. 'Are you a jealous person, Eddy? Do you know what jealousy means?'

Eddy said nothing.

'Paul's jealous,' Cathy went on. 'He watches me. He hates it when I talk to other men.'

Suddenly she smiled.

'I'm crazy,' she said. 'Why am I telling you all this? You're a reporter. A rat. You're my enemy.'

'You're wrong, Miss Chen,' Eddy said. 'I'm not your enemy. I want to be your friend. I'll never write anything bad about you, I promise.'

Cathy sighed.

'Can I trust you?' she said sadly. 'I wish —'

Eddy shut his eyes for a moment.

'But you *can* trust me,' he said.

Cathy laughed.

'This is strange!' she said. 'I will trust you. And anyway, I don't have a choice. I need your help.'

She moved closer to him. Eddy felt her breath on his face.

'I had a maid, Su Lin,' Cathy said. 'She was no good. I told her to leave. Now she hates me. She wants to ruin my life. She has some photos of me with another man. This man is not my fiancé.'

Cathy looked out at the ocean. The silvery moonlight shone on the sea and it shone on her face.

'This man was an old friend,' Cathy said. 'He came to one of my parties. He asked me to dance. He held me very close, and then – then he kissed —'

She stopped speaking. A tear fell from her eye and onto her cheek. Eddy wanted to wipe the tear from her cheek.

'I – I pushed the man away,' Cathy Chen whispered, 'but I wasn't fast enough. Su Lin was there. She had a camera and she took some photos of me and the man. Now she wants to sell them to a newspaper. What can I do? If my fiancé sees the pictures, he'll —'

'Cathy Chen needs me,' Eddy thought. 'Cathy Chen is in trouble. She's asking me to help her.'

'Can't you buy the photos? Pay Su Lin for the photos,' he said. 'Don't you have enough money?'

'Yes, I have enough money,' Cathy said. 'I tried to buy the photographs from Su Lin, but she refused to sell them. She doesn't only want the money. She wants to ruin my life!'

Eddy thought quickly. He had to help Cathy!

'Listen,' he said at last. 'I'll go and see this woman. I'll tell her, "My newspaper wants to buy the photos of Cathy Chen." You give me the money. I'll pay Su Lin. She'll give me the photos and I'll give them to you. Then you can burn the photos.'

'Oh, Eddy,' she said. 'Thank you.'

'Don't worry,' said Eddy. 'Everything will be OK. I'm glad you didn't jump off the rocks!'

'Jump off the rocks?' said Cathy. 'Oh, I wasn't going to jump. I just like being close to the edge. I like dangerous places and I like doing dangerous things.'

'Oh,' said Eddy. 'Well, I *don't* like dangerous places. And I don't like doing dangerous things! So let's go down now!'

5

A Dangerous Woman

'Eddy, you look different today,' Rosita said to Eddy the next morning. 'What happened to you?'

'Mmm?' said Eddy. 'Did you say something? I'm sorry. I wasn't listening.'

Rosita shook her head. 'Eddy is very strange today,' she thought.

Eddy sat at his desk. Above it, on the wall, was Cathy's photograph. Eddy looked at the picture of Cathy Chen and he smiled.

'Good morning, Cathy,' he whispered.

Eddy stared at the phone. He had to speak to Su Lin. 'She has to sell Cathy's photos to the *Daily News*,' he said to himself.

'Eddy!' Rosita called out. 'Mr Lee wants to see you.'

Eddy went into Mr Lee's office.

'Hello, Eddy,' Mr Lee said. 'Sit down. I've just had an interesting phone call from a woman called Su Lin. She was Cathy Chen's maid. She has some photographs of Cathy Chen. I want you to go and see Su Lin. Have a look at the photographs. If they're good, pay Su Lin one thousand dollars. If they're really interesting pictures, pay her ten thousand.'

Eddy looked at the floor.

'I have to be careful,' he thought. 'I have to help Cathy.'

'Did the woman give her address, sir?' he asked Mr Lee. 'Shall I go and see her now?'

'Yes, of course!' said Mr Lee. 'Here is the address – on this piece of paper. Here is a cheque from the *Daily News*. I've signed it already. Agree a price with this woman for the pictures and write the amount on the cheque. Now take a taxi and go to her house as quickly as you can. She's probably phoning other newspapers as well. You have to be there first.'

Eddy stood up and went to the door.

'Eddy,' Mr Lee said. 'If you do this job well, we'll talk about your promotion. Yes, if you get those photographs for the *Daily News*, I'll promote you!'

Eddy ran out of the office and got into a taxi. He told the driver Su Lin's address.

'Promotion! A better job!' he thought. 'Perhaps I will

get a car – and my work would be more interesting too. But what about Cathy? If the photographs are in the *Daily News*, Cathy will be very unhappy. No, I can't do it! I must get the photos and give them to her.'

The taxi stopped outside a small house in the Western Addition. 'Wait for me here, please,' Eddy told the driver.

A woman was watching from a window of the house. She opened the door before Eddy reached it.

'Yes?' she said. 'What do you want?'

'I'm a reporter. I work for the *Daily News*,' Eddy said.

'Come in,' the woman said.

Eddy followed her into a small room. The room was dark and very untidy.

'Do you have the photographs?' asked Eddy. 'My editor will pay you a very good price if —'

'If they're interesting, I guess,' Su Lin said. 'Yes, they're interesting pictures. They're very interesting. Look at them!'

Su Lin opened a drawer in a table and took out the photos. Eddy looked at the first photo. It showed Cathy Chen with a young man. He was holding her in his arms. Eddy looked at the other photos quickly. He didn't like to see another man holding Cathy Chen.

Su Lin pointed to a date on the photograph. 'See the date on that photo? My camera always prints the date on photos,' she said. 'I took this photo less than a year ago. Cathy Chen was engaged to Paul Kwok *before* this picture was taken!'

'I'll give you five thousand dollars for the photos,' Eddy said. 'They're very dark and they are not clear.'

'Five thousand dollars?' the woman said. 'Is that all? I

want twenty thousand dollars! I won't sell the photos for less than twenty thousand.'

'Seven thousand, five hundred dollars,' said Eddy.

'Fifteen thousand,' said Su Lin.

'Ten thousand dollars,' said Eddy. 'No more.'

Su Lin stood up. She walked to the door and held it open. 'No, I won't sell them for that price,' she said.

Suddenly a phone rang in another room.

'Another newspaper is calling!' Eddy thought. He was worried.

Su Lin went to answer the phone.

Eddy waited. He could hear Su Lin speaking, but he could not hear the words. A baby was crying loudly upstairs.

At last Su Lin returned. She was angry.

'OK,' she said. 'I'll sell the photos to you for ten thousand dollars. Now give me the money and get out of here.'

Eddy said nothing for a moment. He remembered his promise to help Cathy Chen.

'I can't give Su Lin the cheque from the *Daily News*,' he thought. 'Su Lin will take the cheque to a bank. She'll get the money. Then Mr Lee will know what has happened. He'll ask me for the photos.'

'I can't give you the money now,' Eddy said. 'I don't carry ten thousand dollars in my pocket.'

Su Lin picked the photographs up quickly.

'That was a mistake,' said Eddy to Su Lin. Very quickly, he put his hand in the pocket of his jacket.

Suddenly Su Lin was afraid. 'You've got a gun!' she shouted.

Eddy did not take his hand out of his pocket.

'I want twenty thousand dollars! I won't sell the photos for
less than twenty thousand.'

'OK, go and get the money,' Su Lin said. 'And I want cash. Be here before four o'clock, or I'll call the *Morning Gazette*. They'll pay more than ten thousand dollars.'

'Be careful, Miss Su Lin,' Eddy told her. 'Don't trick me. I'll come back at four o'clock, with ten thousand dollars. If I find another reporter here, I'll shoot him.'

He ran out of Su Lin's horrible little house. The taxi was still waiting for him. He got into it.

'Where do you want to go now?' the driver said.

'I don't know. Drive for a few minutes, please,' Eddy said.

As the taxi drove through the city, Eddy thought quickly. 'I need ten thousand dollars now. I can go to Cathy's house. But what will happen if Paul Kwok is there?'

Eddy decided to call Cathy Chen first. He took his mobile phone out of his jacket pocket and dialled Cathy Chen's number.

A woman's voice answered the phone.

'Can I speak to Miss Chen, please?' Eddy asked.

'Who's calling?' the woman said.

'My name is Eddy Nakamura,' said Eddy. 'Miss Chen knows me. I'm a friend of hers.'

'One moment, please,' the woman said. 'I'll ask if she'll speak to you.'

Eddy waited. He wanted to hear Cathy's voice. At last she spoke.

'Eddy,' she said. 'Is that you – my favourite rat?'

'Yes,' said Eddy. 'I've seen —'

'Where are you?' Cathy said quickly.

'The Western Addition,' Eddy said. 'Near Su Lin's house. I must have a lot of cash – before four o'clock.'

'How much money?' asked Cathy.

'Ten thousand dollars,' Eddy said. 'It's a lot of money. I'm sorry.'

Cathy laughed.

'If we can stop Su Lin, ten thousand dollars is not a lot of money,' she said. 'Well done, Eddy. Go to Stow Lake in Golden Gate Park. My driver will meet you there. He'll give you the money. I only met you yesterday, but you won't trick me. I'm sure of that.'

'Of course I won't trick you!' said Eddy. 'I —'

'I have to go now,' Cathy said. 'Good luck, Eddy.'

Eddy put his phone back in his pocket. 'Take me to Golden Gate Park, please, driver,' he said.

There was a lot of traffic. At last, the taxi arrived at the entrance to Golden Gate Park.

Eddy looked at his watch. It was nearly two o'clock.

'I'll be late!' thought Eddy.

He jumped out of the taxi and ran through the park towards Stow Lake.

At first Eddy could not see Cathy's driver. A bride and a bridegroom were standing by the water. A photographer was taking their wedding pictures. There were a lot of people by the lake.

Then suddenly Eddy saw Cathy's driver. He was sitting under a tree, and he was reading a magazine. Eddy went towards him.

'Hi,' said Eddy.

The driver looked up.

'Hello again,' the driver said. 'You only met Miss Chen yesterday. You really are amazing. All the reporters try to speak to Cathy Chen. She never speaks to any of them.

Why did she choose you?'

Eddy laughed. 'Do you have an envelope for me?' he asked.

The driver put his hand inside his jacket and pulled out a large white envelope. He gave it to Eddy.

Eddy took the envelope and walked away.

Eddy caught a bus outside the park. He sat at the back of the bus. Then he opened the white envelope. Inside it there were a hundred $100 banknotes – ten thousand dollars!

———

At five minutes to four, Eddy returned to Su Lin's house. She was waiting at her window. Su Lin opened the door but she did not say hello. She did not look at Eddy.

'Give me the money,' she said.

'No,' said Eddy. 'First I want the photos.'

Su Lin went to the table and took a brown envelope out of the drawers. She gave the envelope to Eddy and he opened it. He counted the photographs in the envelope.

'You showed me six photos this morning,' he said. 'There are only five here. And where are the negatives?'

Su Lin said nothing. Eddy ran to the table.

There were two more photographs in the drawer, and some negatives.

'You're trying to trick me,' he said. 'You're keeping some photographs for yourself. You want to sell some of the photos to me and some of them to the *Morning Gazette*. My editor will not like that. He gets angry very easily. And he has some very dangerous friends.'

Su Lin was frightened.

'I'm sorry,' she said. She was breathing fast.

'Is this all of them?' said Eddy. 'Tell me the truth.'

'Yes, yes!' Su Lin said quickly. 'You have them all now, I promise! It's the truth!'

Eddy walked to the door with the brown envelope in his hand.

'You leave Miss Chen alone now,' he said. 'No more trouble, or I'll come and see you again. And you'll be very, very sorry!'

Eddy took the white envelope with the money out of his pocket. He threw the envelope on the floor at Su Lin's feet.

Eddy smiled as he left Su Lin's house. He held the brown envelope tightly in his hand. 'I've got the photos!' he thought to himself. 'Cathy will be so happy!'

6

Mr Wu Gives Eddy a Haircut

Eddy got into a cable car. Two men wearing hats also got into the cable car. They were following him.

It was the rush hour. People were leaving their work in shops, factories and offices. The streets were full of cars and buses.

Eddy looked out of the cable car window and thought about Cathy. He did not see the two men behind him.

'Cathy will be so happy when she sees the photos!' Eddy said to himself.

Eddy jumped off the cable car. He walked toward the offices of the *Daily News*. On the way, he saw the barber

Eddy did not see the two men behind him.

shop of his friend, old Mr Wu.

Inside the window of the shop there was a big mirror. The words 'HAIRCUT, SIR?' were written on the mirror in large red letters.

Eddy saw himself in the mirror.

'I look terrible,' he thought. 'My hair is much too long. I don't want to see Cathy with long hair. I need a haircut.'

Old Mr Wu was sweeping the floor when Eddy went into the shop.

'Hi! Mr Wu, it's me!' said Eddy.

'Oh, hi, Eddy!' Mr Wu said. 'Good to see you. You want a haircut? Say, your hair is long, Eddy.'

'Yes, I guess it is,' Eddy said.

Mr Wu had known Eddy for many years. Eddy always had his hair cut at Mr Wu's shop.

Eddy sat down in the barber's chair in front of a mirror. Mr Wu tied a large towel round Eddy's neck. Eddy was still holding the photographs of Cathy in the brown envelope.

The old man began to cut Eddy's hair.

'Now then,' he said. 'Tell me the news from the news-paper. News from the newspaper, eh? That's funny, isn't it?'

'Yes, very funny,' Eddy said politely. Mr Wu made the same joke every time Eddy came to the barber's shop.

Ten minutes later, Eddy's hair was short and tidy again.

'That's better,' said Mr Wu. 'Now, do you want —'

The door of the barber shop suddenly opened and two men came in. One of them was very tall. They were both wearing hats and sunglasses.

'I'm sorry,' Mr Wu said. 'The shop is closed now. This is my last customer.'

'That's OK,' the tall man said. 'I don't need a haircut.

'That's better,' said Mr Wu.

And my friend here doesn't need one. Show him your head, Ivan.'

The man called Ivan took off his hat. He had no hair on his head. He was bald.

'What do you want?' said Mr Wu.

The men did not look friendly.

'It's OK, old man,' said the tall man. 'We just want to talk to Mr Nakamura.'

Ivan said, 'We want to take Mr Nakamura for a ride.'

Ivan put his hand on Eddy's arm. 'Come with us, Mr Nakamura,' he said.

Eddy looked up at him. Ivan was not smiling.

'He wants the photographs of Cathy,' Eddy thought. 'Who do these men work for? Su Lin?'

'OK, I'll come,' he said. 'Let me pay Mr Wu.'

Eddy's hands were still covered by the big white towel. He put one hand into his pocket and took out ten dollars. He gave the money to Mr Wu. Then, with his other hand, Eddy pulled the towel away from his neck and threw it down on the floor.

'Are you taking me somewhere nice?' he asked.

'Don't try to be funny,' the bald man said.

The two men pushed Eddy out of the shop. Eddy looked back. Mr Wu was watching them. He had not touched the towel. It was lying on the floor. He had not seen the envelope. It was inside the towel.

The men pushed Eddy into a car. They began to drive fast through the city.

Eddy felt cold and his mouth was dry.

'Are they going to hurt me?' he thought. 'Are they going to kill me?'

The car stopped outside some big gates. Eddy knew where they were. It was 3Com Park, the stadium where the San Francisco Giants baseball team and the Forty-Niners football team play.

The two men pulled Eddy out of the car. The big gates of 3Com Park were shut. Ivan unlocked a small door in the wall. The other man pushed Eddy through the door.

Eddy looked round. The stadium was empty.

'Why have you brought me here?' Eddy said.

'We're asking the questions,' the tall man said. 'Now, why are you so interested in Miss Chen? Why did you meet her at the beach? Her driver gave you an envelope. What was inside it?'

The tall man took his hat and sunglasses off. Now Eddy could see his face clearly.

'Wait a minute,' Eddy said. 'I've seen you before. You're Lenny Rivers. You were a football player. You used to play for the Forty-Niners. I saw you play when I was a kid.'

'We're not here to talk about football,' Lenny said.

'We've got a message for you,' said Ivan. 'It's from Mr Kwok.'

'So you work for Mr Kwok?' said Eddy.

'That's right,' said Ivan. 'We're his friends. Mr Kwok doesn't like people following his fiancée. You're a reporter aren't you? Well, listen to this. Mr Kwok doesn't like to read lies about his fiancée in the newspapers. He hates reporters.'

'No, no!' said Eddy. 'You don't understand. I —'

'Then why did you go to Su Lin's house?' Lenny Rivers said.

Eddy said, 'This is crazy. I —'

'Mr Kwok doesn't think it's crazy,' Ivan said. 'He gets angry when people upset Miss Chen. And Mr Kwok is not nice when he's angry.'

Eddy said nothing.

'When you came out of Su Lin's house,' Lenny Rivers said, 'you had an envelope in your hand.'

'You were there?' said Eddy, surprised.

'We followed you,' Ivan said.

He suddenly pushed Eddy hard.

'What were you doing there?' he asked. 'What was in that envelope? What did Su Lin give you? Letters? Stories about Miss Chen?'

Eddy looked down at his feet.

'What envelope?' he said. 'I don't know what you're talking about.'

'You're lying,' Lenny Rivers said. 'Search him, Ivan.'

Lenny Rivers held Eddy's right arm and pulled it up behind his back. Eddy tried to get free but he could not. The tall man was too strong.

Ivan looked in Eddy's pockets, and inside his shirt.

'This is crazy!' Eddy said.

Ivan finished searching him.

'It's not here,' he said.

'Do you believe me now?' Eddy said. 'I was not lying. I don't have an envelope!'

'There *was* an envelope,' Lenny Rivers said. He pulled Eddy's arm up higher.

'Aah!' Eddy shouted. 'You'll break my arm!'

'What did you do with the envelope?' said Lenny. 'Tell me, or I'll break both your arms.'

'OK, I'll tell you,' he said. 'Stop pulling my arm and I'll

'Search him, Ivan.'

tell you.'

Lenny dropped Eddy's arm.

'I – I left the envelope in the taxi,' Eddy said. 'It's not important. There's nothing in it. I forgot about it.'

Lenny held Eddy's arm. He began to pull it up again.

'You're lying!' Lenny shouted. 'Tell us the truth!'

Suddenly there was a noise at one of the gates of the stadium. Someone was opening it. Voices came from the street outside.

'It's the security guards,' Lenny said.

'This is my chance! I must escape now!' Eddy thought.

Eddy pulled his arm away from Lenny. He ran towards the stadium gate. It was open now. Two security guards were coming in. Eddy ran out. Lenny and Ivan followed him.

'Hey!' shouted a security guard. 'Stop! All of you, stop!'

Suddenly, Eddy saw a taxi. It had stopped on the other side of the road. People were getting out of the taxi. Eddy ran across the road. Cars stopped and drivers shouted. Eddy jumped into the taxi. He shut the door and the taxi drove away.

'Thank goodness,' Eddy thought. 'I'm safe!'

7

The Envelope

Eddy went back to Mr Wu's barber shop. The shop was shut. It was dark and empty.

'I must get inside,' thought Eddy. 'I must find Cathy's photographs. Perhaps I can get into the shop at the back.'

Eddy went down a small alley beside the shop. At the end of the alley he turned right into a narrow street with many old buildings. He found the back door of the barber's shop.

The door was locked. There was a small window near the door. The window was shut, but it was not locked. He pushed the window and suddenly it opened.

Eddy looked behind him. The street was empty.

He looked at the window. It was quite high up.

'I'll have to stand on something,' Eddy thought.

Eddy found a garbage can. He pulled it over to the window and stood on it.

It was difficult for Eddy to climb through the small window. He twisted and turned his body. His head was through the window now, and so were his arms. But his legs were still outside.

Eddy kicked his legs. He had to get in! He had to find the photographs! His foot touched something. Then there was a loud noise. The garbage can had fallen over.

'People will hear me!' Eddy thought. 'They'll catch me!'

He pushed and pushed, and suddenly, he was inside the barber's shop. He fell onto the floor of a storeroom. He

He had to get in!

sat there for a moment in the darkness. There were voices outside. People had heard the noise. They had opened their windows. They were looking down into the street.

'It was only a cat,' he heard someone say. 'Look, it's pushed over old Mr Wu's garbage can again.'

Quietly, Eddy stood up. He found a door. He opened it. He was in the front room of the barber's shop now.

Eddy looked around the room. He could not see the towel. He could not see the envelope either.

'I guess Mr Wu swept the floor before he shut the shop,' Eddy thought.

There was a desk with a phone on it near the door.

'Perhaps he put the envelope there,' Eddy thought.

He went over to the desk. There was nothing on it. But there was a drawer in the desk. The drawer was locked.

Suddenly, Eddy heard a noise. Someone was moving about upstairs. He could hear footsteps. Now the person was coming down the stairs, into the shop!

Eddy looked around. The footsteps were closer now. The door into the shop was opening! Eddy quickly hid under the desk.

'Who's there?' said an old man's voice. It was Mr Wu. 'I know someone is there. I heard you!'

Mr Wu stood still for a moment.

'It's that cat again,' Mr Wu said at last. 'I'll have to speak to the neighbours about it. It is always coming in here. Noisy, dirty ...'

Mr Wu's voice was getting quieter. He was going back up the stairs.

Eddy waited for a long time. Then he stood up.

Where was the envelope?

'Perhaps Mr Wu has taken the envelope upstairs,' thought Eddy. 'Or perhaps it's here, in this drawer. I have to find the key.'

Eddy thought for a moment.

He put his fingers under the desk and he felt underneath. Nothing. Then Eddy put his fingers along the shelf above the desk. The key was there!

The drawer unlocked easily. Eddy found the envelope at once. All the photographs were there.

Suddenly, he heard a knock on the shop door. He looked up. Through the glass window in the door he could see two men. One man was very tall. The other man was shorter. Both men were wearing hats.

'Lenny and Ivan!' Eddy thought. 'They didn't believe my story about the taxi. Now they know the truth. They have come for the envelope!'

Lenny and Ivan knocked on the shop door again.

Quickly, Eddy locked the drawer and put the key back on the shelf. Then he ran to the back of the shop and went into the storeroom. As he shut the door behind him, he heard Mr Wu's feet on the stairs again.

'What is all this noise?' Mr Wu was saying. 'Who wants a haircut now? Stop banging on the door. You'll break the glass!'

The back door to the shop was locked on the inside, but the key was in the lock. Eddy opened the door, and went out into the street. Then he began to run.

8

'I Don't Want to Make Trouble'

When Eddy opened the door of his apartment, the phone was ringing. It stopped before he could answer it.

Eddy turned back and locked his front door.

'Lenny and Ivan will follow me here,' he thought. 'They won't stop until they have the photographs. What am I going to do? I must hide the envelope.'

Eddy took a big book from a bookshelf. He opened the book and put the envelope inside it. Then he shut the book and put it back on the shelf.

Eddy began to walk up and down the room. 'What shall I do next?' he thought. He walked up and down again.

'I must speak to Cathy,' he said to himself. 'I must give her the photographs. But she never answers the phone herself. What will happen if Paul Kwok answers?'

A car stopped in the street outside.

'Lenny and Ivan,' he thought. 'How did they find me so quickly?'

Suddenly Eddy knew what to do. He dialled Cathy Chen's number.

A deep voice answered at once.

'Kwok here,' it said.

Eddy shut his eyes for a moment. His heart was beating fast.

'This is Eddy Nakamura,' he said. 'I want to speak to you, Mr Kwok.'

Eddy heard someone open the front door of the apartment building.

'Why are your friends following me, Mr Kwok?' Eddy went on. 'What do you want?'

'I will tell you what I want,' Paul Kwok said. His voice was angry. 'I want you to leave Cathy Chen alone. Do you understand?'

'No,' said Eddy. 'I do *not* understand. I have never hurt Miss Chen.'

'I don't believe you,' Paul Kwok said. 'You are a reporter. All reporters make trouble.'

Eddy could hear footsteps outside his door.

'You're wrong, Mr Kwok,' Eddy said. 'I don't want to

make trouble for Miss Chen. I only want an interview with her for the *Daily News* colour magazine. I – I like Miss Chen very much. She is a lovely person. I will never write anything bad about her.'

'Then why did you go to see Su Lin?' Paul Kwok asked.

Eddy thought quickly. 'Su Lin called me at the offices of the *Daily News*,' he said. 'She wanted me to write about your fiancée. Su Lin wanted me to write lies about her. I met Miss Chen. I asked her about Su Lin. "Don't listen to her," Miss Chen said. "Su Lin is angry because she lost her job. She'll tell you lies." But I'm a reporter, Mr Kwok. I wanted to know the truth. I went to see Su Lin myself. I knew immediately that Miss Chen had told the truth. Su Lin *does* tell lies. I didn't believe her story. I will not tell her story in the newspaper.'

Now Lenny and Ivan were knocking on Eddy's door.

'Your friends are outside my apartment, Mr Kwok,' Eddy said. 'Will you speak to them?'

'But the envelope!' Paul Kwok said. 'What was in it?'

'The envelope?' said Eddy. 'Why are you so interested in the envelope? It was an old envelope from the office. I wrote Su Lin's address on it. And I wrote the directions to her house. I took the envelope with me when I went to see her. Then I left it in the taxi.'

Paul Kwok said nothing.

'Listen, Mr Kwok,' Eddy said. 'I'm not going to write anything bad about Miss Chen. But you must be careful. You were a tennis star. The newspapers have always said kind words about you. But things could easily change —'

Lenny and Ivan were knocking harder on the door. They were shouting Eddy's name.

'Wait a moment, Mr Kwok,' Eddy said. 'I'm going to open my door. I don't want your friends to break the door down.'

Eddy opened the door. Lenny and Ivan stood outside.

'Come in,' Eddy said. 'Mr Kwok wants to speak to you.' And he gave the phone to Lenny.

Lenny listened for a long time. Then he turned to Eddy.

'I'm sorry,' Lenny said. 'We made a mistake. We didn't hurt you, did we? We only wanted —'

'You wanted to help your friend,' Eddy finished the sentence for Lenny. 'It's OK, but please leave now.'

'Oh, sure, we'll go,' Ivan said. 'We're very sorry —'

Eddy opened the door.

'Goodbye,' he said.

And they left.

Suddenly, Eddy was hungry. He went into his little kitchen and found some rice and a few vegetables. He began to cook his supper.

He put the food on the table and sat down to eat. At that moment, someone knocked at the door.

'Oh, no,' thought Eddy. 'Not again!'

He went to the door and opened it.

'Now listen,' he said. 'I told you —'

Then he stopped. Lenny and Ivan and were not standing outside. It was Eddy's boss, Mr Lee.

'Oh, hello, Mr Lee,' said Eddy. 'Come in.'

Mr Lee came in.

'Hello, Eddy,' he said. 'You didn't come back to the office this afternoon. I tried to call you many times. Why didn't you answer? Have you got a good story about Cathy Chen?'

9

'Do You Think I'm a Fool?'

'Please, Mr Lee,' Eddy said. 'Sit down. Would you like a drink? It's very nice to see you. I —'

He did not know what he was saying. He needed time to think.

'I don't want a drink,' Mr Lee said. 'I only want to know what happened with Cathy Chen's maid.'

'Well —' said Eddy.

'I know that you have the photos,' Mr Lee said.

'How did you know that?' Eddy said. He was surprised.

'The editor of the *Morning Gazette* called me,' said Mr Lee. 'He also sent a reporter to see Su Lin. But you were there first. You bought the photos. The *Morning Gazette* is very disappointed. They want to buy some of the photos from us. They'll pay thousands of dollars! I can't wait to see the photos. What's the matter, Eddy?'

'I – I'm sorry, Mr Lee,' Eddy said. 'There are no photos.'

'What!' Mr Lee shouted. 'What do you mean?'

'I went to Su Lin's house,' Eddy said. 'I talked to her. She's an awful woman, Mr Lee. I don't think —'

'I don't care what you think!' said Mr Lee.

'Sir, Su Lin showed me some photos of Cathy Chen,' Eddy went on. He was trying to think of a good story to tell Mr Lee, but he was tired. He could not think fast enough.

'Yes?' Mr Lee asked. 'And?'

'They weren't interesting photos at all!' Eddy said. 'They showed Cathy Chen with her dog. That was all!

47

They were very bad photographs. You couldn't see her face clearly.'

'Oh.' Mr Lee was disappointed. 'What did you do?'

'Well, sir,' Eddy said. 'I was angry. I told Su Lin, "These photos are no good. No one wants these. Burn them. They're garbage." She was angry with me. "You fool," she said. "The *Morning Gazette* will pay me at least a thousand dollars for them." I told her, "You are crazy. The photos aren't worth more than fifty dollars." She said to me, "Then give me fifty dollars." '

'Did you give her fifty dollars?' asked Mr Lee.

'Well, yes, sir,' Eddy said.

'So where are the photos, Eddy?' asked Mr Lee.

'I don't have them, sir,' Eddy said. 'They were so bad, I put them in – in the garbage can.'

'What?' Mr Lee said. 'You paid for those photos with fifty dollars of the *Daily News*' money, then you put the photos in the garbage can? Do you think I'm a fool, young man?'

'But sir! It wasn't the *Daily News*' money,' said Eddy. 'Su Lin wanted cash. So I gave her fifty dollars of my own money. Here's your cheque, sir.'

Eddy gave the cheque to Mr Lee.

Mr Lee's face was very red. He stood up angrily.

'Eddy,' Mr Lee said. 'I wanted to promote you. I wanted to give you some bigger assignments. I'm disappointed. I gave you your chance. But you're a fool.'

'But, Mr Lee,' Eddy said. 'Those photographs were no good —'

'It's not only the photographs,' said Mr Lee. 'You had a chance to talk to Cathy Chen's maid. You had a chance to get a really good story. Su Lin worked for Cathy Chen for more than a year. She must know a lot about her. Su Lin doesn't like Cathy Chen. Why didn't you interview her?'

'A maid who hates her employer doesn't tell the truth!' Eddy said. 'Is that what you want? Do you want lies?'

Mr Lee turned to the door.

'You're a fool, Eddy,' he said. 'I won't forget this. You won't write news articles again. You will stay and work in the office every day. The girl who answers the readers' letters left the *Daily News* today. You will take her job tomorrow morning.'

Mr Lee went out of the door. Eddy heard him leaving the apartment building.

'Answering readers' letters!' Eddy thought. 'The worst job in the office!'

He was very unhappy. He looked at his supper. It was cold. Anyway he was not hungry now. He took the plate into the kitchen and put the food into the garbage can.

'I'm a fool!' he thought. 'Why did I do all this for Cathy Chen? She doesn't care about me at all!'

Eddy wanted to run after Mr Lee. He wanted to tell him the truth. Eddy had tried to help Cathy Chen. He had made a mistake. He wanted to give the chief editor the photographs and see him smile.

But then Eddy thought of Cathy's beautiful face. He went to the window and pressed his face against the cool glass.

'I *am* a fool,' he thought. 'A stupid, stupid fool.'

Outside, it was nearly dark. Eddy looked at the lights of San Francisco.

The phone rang.

'I am *a* fool. A *stupid, stupid fool.*'

'Eddy? Is that you?' said a soft voice.

'Cathy!' he whispered. 'Oh, Cathy! I —'

'Do you have the photos?' Cathy asked.

'Yes,' said Eddy, 'but it was very —'

'I can't talk now,' Cathy said. 'My aunt is here. Meet me at the Golden Gate Bridge. Meet me tomorrow evening at six o'clock. Goodnight, Eddy. Sweet dreams!'

'Wait, Cathy! Listen!' said Eddy.

There was a click from the phone. Then there was silence. Cathy had gone.

10

'Friends Are Very Important'

The next day, Eddy started his new job at the *Daily News*. He hated it. He hated answering readers' letters. The other reporters were sorry for him.

'I can't do this!' Eddy said to Rosita at lunch time. 'I can't answer readers' letters. I want to be a news reporter. I'll go crazy!'

'Listen, Eddy,' Rosita said quietly. 'Mr Lee is very angry. So just do what he says now. Work on the readers' letters. Perhaps Mr Lee will give you another chance one day.'

Rosita was right. Eddy knew this. He worked on his boring job all day. At last, he had finished all the letters. Then he quickly returned home to get Cathy's photos. He put them in his pocket and went to meet Cathy.

Eddy was late. He did not arrive at the Golden Gate Bridge until after six-thirty.

Cathy's white limousine was in the car park, but Eddy could not see Cathy. The driver was sitting inside the car. He was listening to the radio.

'Hi,' Eddy said. 'Where's Miss Chen?'

The man pointed to the path that led to the top of the cliffs nearby.

'She went for a walk along the Marin Headlands,' he said. 'She's up there on the top of the cliff!'

'Why did you let her go alone?' said Eddy. 'It can be dangerous up there.'

The man smiled.

'You don't know Miss Cathy Chen,' he said. 'She does what she wants to do. She likes to go for walks alone. I can't stop her.'

Eddy began to run up the cliff path. He was worried.

'Why does Cathy like to come here?' he thought. 'It's not safe.'

The path was steep. Eddy climbed as quickly as he could. The path went up to the top of the cliff and then along the cliff edge. He could see the rocks at the bottom of the cliff. And beyond them was the sea.

Eddy could see something else, too. A woman in a blue dress was sitting on the edge of the cliff. Her black hair was flying in the wind. Her legs were hanging over the edge of the cliff. The rocks were far, far below.

'Cathy!' shouted Eddy.

She turned to him and waved her hand.

Eddy walked towards her. He was closer to her now, and he was closer to the edge of the cliff. It was very high here. He did not want to go closer. He was afraid of high places. He was afraid of falling.

'Cathy, don't sit there!' Eddy said. 'It's too dangerous.'

Cathy laughed.

'I told you, I like heights. I like danger,' she said. 'Do you have the photographs? Give them to me quickly.'

'No,' said Eddy. 'I won't give you anything until you come away from the edge of the cliff.'

Cathy jumped up. Eddy shut his eyes. She was going to fall! Then suddenly she was standing beside him.

'Please, sweet Eddy,' she said. 'Give me the photos.'

He took the envelope out of his pocket and gave it to her. She looked at the photographs.

'What a fool!' she said.

She began to tear the photos into small pieces. Then she held her hands up and opened them. The wind blew the pieces away, over the edge of the cliff.

Eddy turned and looked at Cathy. Her blue dress was the same colour as the sky. She was laughing happily.

'Cathy,' he said. 'Listen. I —'

She turned towards him. 'Yes?' she said.

'Cathy, you're unhappy with Paul,' Eddy went on. 'I know this.'

He stopped speaking. Cathy Chen did not look at him.

'Cathy, I will do anything for you,' Eddy said. 'Paul Kwok will never make you happy. But I —'

Cathy turned towards him. Her face was angry.

'Stop this, Eddy,' she said. 'Don't speak about Paul like that!'

'Why not?' Eddy said. 'You don't love him. You're frightened of him. You paid ten thousand dollars for those photographs.'

Cathy pushed her hair back from her face.

The wind blew the pieces away, over the edge of the cliff.

'You don't understand anything, Eddy!' she said. 'I *love* Paul. He's a wonderful man. He's strong. He's clever. He looks after me.'

'But – but I heard you shouting and —' began Eddy.

'We do shout at each other sometimes,' Cathy went on. 'Everybody shouts and screams sometimes. I shout at him. He shouts at me.' She smiled. 'I shouted and screamed at him a lot a few days ago. I wanted to learn to fly. Paul wouldn't let me. "It's too dangerous," he said. I was so angry! "You're cruel," I told him. "I love heights. I love planes!" '

'I understand,' Eddy said. 'You don't care about me. You only wanted those photos. So you were nice to me.'

He began to walk back down the cliff path. Cathy ran after him.

'Hey!' she said. 'Don't be angry, Eddy. I *do* care about you. But I don't love you. You are my friend. I didn't want Paul to see the photographs! I didn't want him to be unhappy. And I am *not* frightened of him.'

She stopped and turned to look at the ocean again.

'I want to have friends,' Cathy said. 'And I want to be your friend. Believe me, Eddy, friends are very important.'

'I'm sorry —' Eddy said.

'I'm sorry too,' said Cathy. 'I wanted those photos back. I didn't think about you. But I'm going to marry Paul, Eddy. I love Paul.'

They walked back to the car park. They did not speak. Cathy Chen's driver opened the back door of the white limousine.

'Can we drive you home?' said Cathy.

'No thanks,' Eddy said. 'I just want to be alone.'

He walked by the ocean for a long time. Soon it was completely dark. The moon made a silver path across the water.

Eddy sat on a rock and listened to the sound of the ocean.

'I'm a fool,' he thought. 'Of course Cathy Chen doesn't love me.'

Slowly, he began to walk back across the bridge towards the lights of San Francisco.

11

Eddy Gets Another Chance

The next few weeks were difficult for Eddy.

'What's the matter, Eddy?' Rosita said one morning.

Eddy sighed.

'I hate answering these letters,' he said. 'Mr Lee is still angry with me. He'll never give me another chance to be a news reporter. Perhaps I'll try to get a job at the *Gazette*.'

At that moment, the phone rang.

'Is that Eddy?' a voice said. 'Is that my favourite rat?'

Eddy knew that voice at once.

'Cathy?' he said.

'Come to my house for lunch,' said Cathy. 'There is something Paul and I want to tell you. My driver will come and get you at twelve o'clock.'

The morning passed slowly. Eddy tried to work. He was watching the clock. The minutes went by very slowly.

At last it was twelve o'clock.

'Are you going out to get a sandwich?' Rosita asked him. 'Can you get me one?'

'I'm sorry, Rosita,' said Eddy. 'I can't today. I'm having lunch with someone.'

'Ah,' said Rosita. 'A secret girlfriend.'

Eddy smiled sadly.

'No,' he said. 'She's just a friend.'

Outside, in the street, Cathy's limousine was waiting for him. Eddy sat in the back.

'Oh – it's you again!' the driver said.

The big gates of Cathy Chen's house opened as the car came near. When the limousine stopped, Eddy got out. He ran up the steps of the house. A maid opened the front door.

'Follow me, sir,' the maid said.

Eddy followed her into a big, beautiful room. There were expensive Chinese rugs on the floor and beautiful flowers on every table.

Cathy and Paul were sitting on a sofa together. They were holding hands. Cathy stood up when she saw Eddy.

'Eddy!' she said. 'This is Paul Kwok.'

Paul stood up and shook Eddy's hand.

'We – er – we've spoken to each other on the phone,' Paul said.

'Really?' said Cathy. She was surprised. 'When?'

'It was long time ago,' said Eddy. He smiled at Paul.

'Sit down,' Paul said. 'Cathy has to tell you something.'

'Eddy,' said Cathy. 'Today is a very special day for Paul and me. We're getting married this afternoon. It will be a private wedding. Only our families and a few friends will be there. We don't want TV cameras and newspaper reporters. No one will find out about the wedding until tomorrow. Then Paul and I will be far away in Hawaii. But you are going to tell the story, Eddy! We will send the photographs to you this evening. Only the *Daily News* will have this story! It will be an exclusive story for you!'

Eddy did not arrive back at the office until the middle

of the afternoon. Mr Lee watched him walk in.

'Where have you been?' he said angrily. 'You can't go out whenever you like!'

'I'm sorry, sir,' Eddy said. 'But I had lunch with Cathy Chen and Paul Kwok. They've just given me some big news. They're not telling anyone else. This is an exclusive for the *Daily News*!'

'Really?' said Mr Lee. 'Cathy Chen and Paul Kwok? Come into my office, Eddy, and tell me all about it!'

———

Next morning, Eddy went to the office early. He could not wait to see the newspaper. Rosita was in the office already. She waved a copy of the newspaper at him.

'Well done, Eddy!' she said. 'You're a famous reporter at last!'

Eddy took the newspaper from her. On the front page was a photograph of Cathy and Paul. And underneath it were the words, 'SECRET WEDDING – MOVIE STAR MARRIES TENNIS CHAMPION, A special report by Eddy Nakamura'.

'The front page!' shouted Eddy. 'My name is on the front page!'

Mr Lee came in.

'Well done, Eddy,' he said. 'I was wrong about you. You did a good report on Cathy Chen's wedding. Excellent. Now, I have another assignment for you. The kung fu movie star, Lucky Lo, is going to —'

Eddy spoke quickly.

'I'm sorry, Mr Lee,' he said. 'I don't want to write any more stories about movie stars. I want to write about important things.'

Mr Lee laughed.

'We'll see, Eddy,' he said. 'Perhaps next year, if —'

The phone rang. Rosita answered it.

'This call is for you, Eddy,' she said. 'It's Cathy Chen.'

Eddy took the phone from her and listened. Then he smiled and put the phone down.

'What did she say?' said Mr Lee.

'She said, "I am the happiest woman in the world," ' said Eddy. 'She's going to send me some more photographs in few days' time. Also, she wants me to interview her and her husband when they come home.'

'Eddy! That's fantastic!' said Rosita.

Mr Lee was smiling.

'I know what will happen,' Mr Lee said. 'We'll have another exclusive story about Cathy Chen, on the front page of the *Daily News*. OK, Eddy. Come into my office. We will talk about promotion. I always liked your work. I always said to Rosita, "He's a good reporter." Didn't I, Rosita?'

Rosita tried not to smile.

'Oh, yes, Mr Lee,' she said.

Points for Understanding

1

1 Where does Eddy work?
2 What is his job?
3 Did Eddy want to write about horse-racing or to have a more serious assignment?
4 What did Mr Lee ask Eddy to write about?
5 Was Eddy pleased?
6 What did Rosita think about Eddy's assignment?

2

1 Did Eddy speak to Cathy Chen when he went to her house?
2 How did Eddy get into Cathy Chen's garden?
3 How many voices did Eddy hear?
4 Describe the voices.
5 Who was in the black car?

3

1 Did Eddy write an article about Cathy Chen?
2 Was Mr Lee pleased with Eddy's article?
3 What did Mr Lee say to Eddy?
4 Why did Eddy go to the White Nights club?
5 Where did Cathy Chen's driver tell Eddy to go?

4

1 What did Cathy Chen climb?
2 Did Eddy like the place?
3 What did Eddy shout to Cathy Chen?
4 What did Cathy Chen call reporters?
5 What did Cathy Chen say to Eddy?
6 Who does Su Lin want to sell the photographs to?

5

1 Where did Mr Lee send Eddy?
2 What did Mr Lee give Eddy?
3 What was printed on the photographs?
4 How much did Eddy pay for the photographs?
5 Su Lin showed Eddy six photographs. How many were
  there in the brown envelope?
6 What did Eddy find in the drawer?

6

1 Who followed Eddy into the cable car?
2 Why did Eddy want a haircut?
3 Who came into the barber shop?
4 Write two of the questions that the men asked Eddy.
5 How did Eddy escape?

7

1 Why did Eddy go back to Mr Wu's barber shop?
2 Where did Eddy find the envelope?
3 Who knocked on the door of the barber shop?

8

1 Who did Eddy phone?
2 What did Eddy ask?
3 Eddy said, 'It was an old envelope from the office.' Was this
  true or a lie?
4 Who knocked on Eddy's door the first time?
5 Who knocked on Eddy's door the second time?

9

1 What did Eddy say to Mr Lee?
2 Did Eddy pay for the photos with the *Daily News'* money?
3 Mr Lee was angry. What did he say to Eddy?
4 Who phoned Eddy?

10

1 What did Eddy hate?
2 What did Rosita say to him?
3 What was Eddy afraid of?
4 What did Cathy Chen do with the photographs?
5 Did Eddy love Cathy Chen? How do you know?
6 Eddy said to Cathy Chen, 'You don't care about me.' Was that true?

11

1 Who invited Eddy to lunch? Why?
2 Had Eddy met Paul Kwok before?
3 What were Cathy Chen and Paul Kwok going to do?
4 Who will have the exclusive story?
5 Did Mr Lee promote Eddy immediately?
6 What did Cathy Chen say on the phone?
7 What did Mr Lee say then?

Macmillan Heinemann English Language Teaching, Oxford

A division of Macmillan Publishers Limited

Companies and representatives throughout the world

ISBN 0 435 27303 5

Editorial development by Phoenix Publishing Services
Illustrated by Bob Harvey
Map on page 4 by John Gilkes
Typography by Adrian Hodgkins
Designed by Sue Vaudin
Cover by Matthew Richardson and Marketplace Design
Typeset in 11.5/14.5pt Goudy
Printed and bound in Spain

99 00 01 02 10 9 8 7 6 5 4 3 2 1